Our Granny

story by MARGARET WILD

pictures by JULIE VIVAS

Houghton Mifflin Company • Boston

First American edition 1994 published by
Houghton Mifflin Company, 222 Berkeley Street,
Boston, Massachusetts 02116

First published in Australia by Omnibus Books

Manufactured in the United States of America

Typography by David Saylor
The text of this book is set in 28 pt. New Baskerville.
The illustrations are watercolor, reproduced in full color.

WOZ   10

Library of Congress Cataloging-in-Publication Data

Wild, Margaret.
    Our Granny / written by Margaret Wild ; illustrated by
Julie Vivas. —1st American ed.
        p.   cm.
    Summary: While grannies come in all shapes and sizes, "our granny"
is unique.
    RNF ISBN 0-395-67023-3   PAP ISBN 0-395-88395-4
    [Grandmothers—Fiction.]
I. Vivas, Julie, ill.   II. Title.
PZ7.W64574Ou   1994
[E] — dc20   93-11950   CIP AC

For Granny Watson
— M. W.

For Alison and Pilar
— J. V.

Some grannies live in . . .

apartments

big old houses

old people's homes

little rooms in the city

trailers

farmhouses

cottages by the ocean

nursing homes

or nowhere at all.

Our granny lives with us in our house.

Some grannies have . . .

thin legs

fat knees

bristly chins

interesting hair

crinkly eyes

friendly smiles

or big soft laps.

Our granny has a wobbly bottom.

Some grannies wear . . .

jeans and sneakers

pantsuits

silky dresses

big bras

baggy underwear

lots of jewelry

high heels

sensible shoes

or comfy slippers.

Our granny wears a funny bathing suit.

Some grannies . . .

baby-sit

drive trucks

fix the plumbing

go to college

travel

write books

work in an office

play in a band

or make sick people better.

Our granny marches in demonstrations.

Some grannies play . . .

cards

tennis

golf

or badminton.

Some grannies . . .

hike

jog

dance

learn t'ai chi

or ride bikes.

Our granny does special exercises
to make her bottom smaller.

Some grannies have . . .

husbands

best friends

cats

dogs

or parakeets.

Some grannies have had three husbands.

Some grannies have had six husbands!

Our grandpa is dead, but our granny often thinks about him.

Sometimes she wears his old red sweater with the holes in the sleeve.

Some grannies . . .

blow kisses

put kisses at the bottoms of their letters

leave lipstick on your cheek

give big sloppy kisses that make your ear wet

or don't kiss much at all.

Our granny always kisses us good night in bed.

Some grannies have . . .

many grandchildren

or even great-grandchildren.

Our granny has us, and we have her.

We love our granny.